THE REPRIEVE

Phil Emmert

The Reprieve

This is a work of fiction. Names, characters, places, and incidents either are products of the author's imagination or are used fictitiously.

First edition 2018

Published in the USA by thewordverve inc.
(www.thewordverve.com)

eBook ISBN: 978-1-948225-65-6
Paperback ISBN: 978-1-948225-66-3

Library of Congress Control Number: 2018914024

~~~~~

The Reprieve

A Book with Verve by *thewordverve inc.*

Cover Design by A.L. Lovell
www.beechhousebooks.com

eBook formatting by Sharyn Bradford Lunn
bradfordlunn@outlook.com

Interior formatting by Bob Houston
www.facebook.com/eBookFormatting/info
~~~~~

TABLE OF CONTENTS

~1~

From Boys to Men

The tall, lanky boy of eighteen folded himself into his dad's 1934 four-door Chevy. He was dressed in blue jeans, flannel shirt, and a denim jacket. His raven black hair was all slicked down with a healthy dab of hair tonic. It was Saturday night, and Tommy Neal was on his way to the Avon Theater in Frankfort to see Clark Gable in a war movie. It was an action-packed movie about American boys joining the Royal Canadian Air Force to fight Germans. He parked at the town square and waved at some of his school buddies who were waiting for him. They bought their tickets and went into the theater together.

Going to a movie was the best way Tommy could relax and unwind after shucking corn by hand all day. The crop was almost all in the crib. Just about twenty more rows to pick. His dad had assigned him to do the picking and shucking after school. He figured he would knock those final rows out by dark on Wednesday.

Tommy loved war movies. America was not in the war over in Europe. But he had heard the teachers at school and the old men at the grain elevator saying we would be in it before long. The Democrats kept saying that Roosevelt would keep us out of the war. Republicans were arguing that we would because the Democrats always got us into war. Now, Tommy didn't know or care anything about politics. But he was thinking that he might enlist in the Canadian Army because they were already involved in the conflict. He just wanted to get off the farm. As the oldest boy in a family of five other siblings, he thought too much of the work fell on him.

Tommy was home by ten thirty that night, a half hour under his curfew. He drank a glass of milk that was fresh from the evening milking and went off to bed. He tried to walk softly so as to not wake his two younger brothers who slept in bunk beds in the same room. Ten-year-old Tim rolled over and asked, "How was the movie?" Tommy just grunted back, "Good. It was good. Now go back to sleep, squirt."

Sunday morning woke the family up to a rooster crowing and one of the cows lowing. Tommy was up and sitting at the kitchen table before the other five siblings came bounding and hollering down the stairs. When they got to the table, they became quiet, as their father, Thomas Sr., frowned at them. Ruth smiled, but said nothing as she stood at the huge wood-fired cook stove.

It was scrambled eggs, homemade cheese biscuits, gravy, and ham. Strong, black coffee was poured into everyone's cup; the little ones got to put cream and sugar in theirs.

Ruth Neal, who was the matriarch, bowed her head, and everyone followed suit. She said a quick prayer for the food and for her family. Her Sunday morning prayer was always short because they would get a large dose of prayer in church.

By nine thirty, all eight Neals were in the car. Ruth and the oldest girl, Donna, sat in front, with Thomas driving. Packed into the back were Tommy, Tim and Theodore, whom everyone called Teddy. The two youngest girls, Jean and Judy, sat on the laps of the boys. This was their regular Sunday morning routine.

They were on their way to Bear Creek Church of Christ, just five miles away. Bear Creek Church was established in 1875, according to the plaque on the corner of the building. It was an old white clapboard, but well-maintained building, with a large black bell, topped off with a steeple pointing to heaven. The building sat at the end of a narrow lane with large oak trees on both sides. For some strange reason there were still hitching posts out front, although no one had driven a horse-drawn carriage to church in more than ten years.

The young preacher was Jake Jennings, just out of Johnson Bible College down in Tennessee. Jake worked at the local glove factory to supplement the seven dollars a week the church paid him. Tommy thought he couldn't preach worth a nickel, but his sermons were short and he was a really friendly and funny guy when he was out of the pulpit. A lot of young people came to church since he had been there. He wasn't married, and some of the teenage girls had their caps set for him. They often made his face turn red when they winked or blew a kiss at him from behind their hymn books while he was preaching.

The message was from the "Sermon on the Mount" that Sunday morning. It was about loving your enemies. Tommy couldn't identify with that because at eighteen years of age, he figured he didn't have an enemy in the world. And he didn't hate anyone. Now there was a fellow or two in his class that he would like to punch out at times. But shucks, he didn't hate them, and they surely were not his enemies.

On Sundays, Thomas Sr. always did the morning chores on his sixty-acre farm. However, he usually required the kids to help with the Sunday evening chores. He and his family had worked hard on that farm to survive what was now being called "The Great Depression." It wasn't over yet, but this year they had dug themselves out of a financial hole with a bumper crop, and the prices were better than they had been in years. Things were beginning to look up.

Back home after church, everyone sat at the large kitchen table. Thomas Sr. sat in the captain's chair at the head of the table. Ruth sat in the stool chair at the other end, with the children lining the benches on either side. On Sundays, the family always lingered a little longer over the huge meal that Ruth had prepared on Saturday evening. After much bantering, the children cleared the table and washed the dishes. Soon they were ready for their Sunday family time. Sunday was set aside for relaxing, reading the paper, playing cards, and checkers. No one could beat Thomas Sr. at checkers ... unless he allowed one of the younger kids to beat him.

On this particular Sunday, which was the first Sunday in December, the younger kids had the new Montgomery Ward catalogue down on the floor. They were using different colored crayons to circle items they wanted for Christmas. Each child had his or her own color. They wouldn't get many of the things they had circled, but they could wish. That's what their mama called the Ward's catalogue—*The Wish Book.*

At about one thirty that afternoon, the telephone on the wall began to ring one long ring. Someone was trying to alert everyone on the party line that there was an emergency in the neighborhood. Might be a fire or someone got hurt. Ruth picked up the receiver and as she listened, a surprised frown came across her face. The voice on the other end was so shrill and loud that it could be heard across the room. After a few seconds, Ruth hung up. Everyone was staring at her. She told Tommy to turn on the radio.

While it was warming up and waiting to come on, she said the Japanese had attacked some place called Pearl Harbor. Just then there was a somber, serious-sounding voice speaking from the large RCA Victor radio that sat on one wall, with a rocking chair next to it. Ruth often sat knitting in that chair while she listened to the stories in the afternoon. Today, Thomas Sr. was sitting in that chair reading the Sunday paper, with the kids sitting on the sofa or sprawled out on the floor.

The voice from the radio said a large group of Japanese fighter planes and bombers had attacked Pearl Harbor on the island of Hawaii. Many ships had been damaged. Thomas Sr. almost to himself and in a very serious tone, said, "This means war." Ruth's face was as white as a sheet and tears were welling up in her eyes. She was remembering her brother who had died in a muddy trench in France in 1918. Tommy had a strange feeling deep down in his gut that things were really going to change in his life. He had planned to graduate from high school in the spring. Now, he didn't know.

The rest of the day was spent by the family in front of that radio or on the phone when they could get an open line. Many calls went back and forth. By dark, all the chores had been done, with even the little ones pitching in without complaining.

On Monday morning at school, nearly all of the boys in the senior class arrived early and congregated out behind the large brick gymnasium. Most of them were smoking cigarettes while they talked about which service they would join. Many wanted to join the Navy since it was the Navy that had mainly suffered so many losses. The causalities were said to be in the hundreds. That was later found to be a low estimate.

Tommy was thinking that he wanted to be in the thick of things. He was going to go for the best. He was going to enlist in the Marines. All the senior boys made a pact. They would enlist as soon as an enlistment office opened up in town. By noon that day, the rumor was that an enlistment office would open up on Wednesday or Thursday.

Also on that Monday, President Roosevelt asked Congress to declare war on not only Japan, but on Germany as well. The Germans had been sinking American ships carrying war supplies to England for several months. The politicians now had a good excuse to declare war on them.

At supper the next night, Tommy made his announcement to the family. He was joining the Marines. His mother shook her head. Thomas Sr. seemed to wince. Then he said, “After you graduate, maybe.”

“No!” Tommy snapped. “This coming Saturday,

all of us in the senior class are going to go enlist." It was settled in Tommy's mind. He was eighteen and a man. He would make his own decisions.

That night, Ruth cried herself into a fitful sleep. Thomas tossed and turned. He finally got up and went to the barn. That barn had served him as a sanctuary through all of his family emergencies. It had been his hiding place where he talked to God while his children were being born and through the darkest days of the depression. Thomas bowed his head on his knees in that barn and prayed. "God, Tom is my oldest. He is my life. Please, God, take care of him." After he prayed, he lay down by Ruth, held her in his arms, and they comforted each other until the rooster crowed.

On Saturday morning, the boys all lined up at the courthouse where the enlistment office had been established. Things were not all that well-organized yet. The line moved slowly. Each boy had to swear that he was at least eighteen years old or accompanied by a parent. Tommy signed several papers and was told he would need to report for a physical on Monday. A room was set up in a downtown empty store building for Army doctors to come and give the physicals.

On Sunday the fourteenth of December, Bear

Creek Church was filled to capacity. The service was somber and very spiritual. Even Jake Jennings, the young preacher, was more serious than normal. At the invitation, several young people came forward. Some came to rededicate their lives. Two young men and two teenage girls made their confession of faith. Since Bear Creek had no baptistery, and there was a skim of ice on the creek, they would be baptized in the neighboring Baptist Church baptistery that afternoon. The Church of Christ believed in same-day baptism for the remission of sins and to receive the gift of the Holy Spirit.

Just after he closed the service with prayer, Preacher Jennings made an announcement. The church would need to find another preacher; he was enlisting in the Army. There were audible moans. He then asked all the men who had already enlisted to stand. The congregation erupted with applause, and some of the ladies began to weep. It was the most emotion that had been shown in that congregation in many years.

There was a long line on Monday at the store building where the physicals were being given. Actually, there were three long lines with a doctor and a nurse at the front of each line. Handing the nurse his papers, Tommy answered a series of questions about childhood diseases and other kinds of embarrassing questions about his life. Tommy weighed in at one hundred sixty-five pounds and he was six feet four inches tall. The doctor said some good ole army food would put some meat on his bones. Tommy shot back, "I'm signing up for the Marines, sir."

After the physical, he was directed to a desk with an older Marine sergeant sitting behind it. Along with his sergeant stripes were several service stripes and a chest full of various ribbons. His face was creased and he reminded Tommy of a neighbor's English bulldog. He thought to himself, *He must be at least a thirty-year man*. He was asked all kinds of questions and had to sign more papers and once again swear that he was at least eighteen years old.

Tommy, along with about fifty or sixty other men, raised their right hand and swore their allegiance to the United States of America and that they would defend America from all enemies foreign or domestic. *Shucks, that was easy. That's why he signed up*.

After this ordeal, he was told to go home. However, he was to report to the bus station Monday after next, at 6:00 a.m. The bus would take those who were joining the Marines all the way to Parris Island, South Carolina for basic training.

Tommy had a week to tell his family and friends goodbye. His mother made a huge meal and invited all the family members to come have a going-away party on Saturday. There were grandparents, aunts, uncles, and cousins present, and it wasn't even Christmas yet. All in all, there were forty-two people present. It was the nicest party Tommy had ever had in his honor. Everyone hugged him before they left, and two cousins told him they were enlisting as soon as they graduated and turned eighteen. His dad's brother, Uncle Johnny, announced that he had already enlisted in the Army. He would be leaving in two weeks.

Monday morning after a tearful goodbye at the bus station, Tommy boarded the olive drab Marine bus along with eighteen other young men. The grizzled old sergeant barked in a loud voice for them to get on board. As the bus moved down the highway, the men grew very quiet, each lost in their own thoughts. They did not seem as bold as they had a week before.

The bus kept moving all through the day and the night. It only paused for restroom breaks and to buy sandwiches. They changed drivers every six hours. They arrived at Parris Island in the wee hours of the morning.

The next week was confusing and loud, with the only quiet time from about 9:00 p.m. until 4:30 a.m. Tommy learned quickly that 9:00 p.m. was 2100 hours and four thirty in the morning was 0430 hours, according to Sergeant Sanders.

Now, Tommy always thought his dad was tough on him. But he couldn't hold a candle to Sergeant Sanders. Tommy always thought he was tough, too. But he found himself next to tears at times and mad as hell at other times.

Marching was not bad. Even the ten-mile hikes were a piece of cake. It was the constant in-your-face barking of Sergeant Sanders and that little bantam rooster, Corporal Jackson, who followed Sanders around, that bothered him.

Finally after a week or so, they got to go to the firing range and qualify with weapons. Tommy found he was an expert shot with all three of the weapons he fired. But since he was so tall and pretty strong, he was issued a BAR, or Browning automatic rifle. It really packed a punch. And in a firefight, he later learned he was happy to have it. One day, Tommy was reading the bulletin board and saw they were looking for a few good men for a unit called the "Raiders." It was an elite group that would be called on for special assignments and to be first into battle. Tommy addressed his desire to be in this special unit to Sergeant Sanders.

At first, Sergeant Sanders tried to talk him out of it. But when he saw Tommy's determination, he took him to Captain McCormick. Captain McCormick looked Tommy up and down, studied a minute, and said, "Okay, trooper, but I will tell you right now, not many men make it through the training."

The next day Tommy was moved to another part of the camp and he began to see what Captain McCormick was talking about. The training seemed twice as intense as before. They often had to fall out at a moment's notice and at all times of the day or night for ten-mile hikes with a full pack and weapons.

One stormy, rain-drenched night they went on such a hike. They were routed out of their bunks at 2300 hours. Loaded down with a full backpack and weapons, they marched for what seemed like seven or eight miles. They were then blindfolded and separated from each other. Corporal Powers instructed Tommy to count slowly to one hundred before taking off the blindfold. The final instruction was to find his way back to the barracks, and he had two hours to be back in front of the barracks.

When the blindfold came off, Tommy found himself all alone. He was somewhat disoriented. Which way to go? There were no stars out. All he could hear was the rain falling. He couldn't see his hand in front of his face. Then there was a lightning flash and he saw the road they had been on. He sure hoped he was picking the right route.

After about a hundred yards, he came across another man in this unit. They agreed that this was the way. About every couple hundred yards, they found a straggler or two, and by 0345 hours, they were assembled in front of their barracks, soaking wet, muddy, and tired but self-satisfied that they had done really good. Sergeant Sanders barked at them that they were ten minutes late! Then he turned smartly on his heel, and walked off smiling. He thought to himself, *Damn, these jarheads are good.*

This intense training lasted another twelve weeks with many more tough tests of strength, endurance, and decision-making in tough situations. There was bayonet practice and what was called hand-to-hand combat, and learning how to kill silently with a stiletto, a combat knife, and other weapons, such as an eighteen-inch coil of piano wire.

Before the twelve weeks was up, several men had washed out. Tommy was proud to be one who finished the course and felt victorious. He was now a "Marine Raider." He was one of the elite.

There was a brief graduation ceremony. But none of Tommy's family were able to come to it. The war effort was in full swing. He wrote a nice letter to the family, telling them all about his new unit and what a great bunch of guys they were.

Two days after they finished basic and specialized training, orders were given that they would be leaving for California soon. Soon was the next day. Several transport airplanes were used to fly them to a small camp not far from San Diego. They were introduced to their new quarters, a dozen rows of squad tents surrounded by woods. They also met their new commanding officer (CO) and his staff. The First Sergeant looked to be only about twenty-five years old. His name was Sam Grant. Three days later, even before they could settle in, they were taken by trucks to the shipyard and loaded onto a troop ship. This was it. They would shortly be doing what they were trained for—killing Japs.

Tommy soon found that time was not a friend. On the ship, he became bored. Each morning, he looked out, and all he could see was blue sky, dark-blue ocean, and other ships in a convoy. He could feel the ship speed up, slow down, and make pretty sharp turns at irregular intervals. The buzz was that they were zigzagging to prevent being torpedoed by Jap subs. With not much to do in tight quarters, tempers sometimes flared. But so far, no one had to be put in the brig for fighting.

Tommy didn't play cards for money or shoot craps, so he mostly read old magazines that the guys exchanged. He tried to write a letter every day or two. But after the first week, there was nothing new to say. He became close buddies with five other guys. They were from different parts of the country and all had quite different experiences. They nicknamed Tommy "country boy" or just "country." That was fine with him. He was proud to be a country boy.

He learned pretty fast that some of the guys in his elite outfit were not as honest and trustworthy as the kids he had been raised with. There were the "tall story tellers." You couldn't believe a word they said. But their stories were good. Some were downright funny. Tommy would sometimes write home about these outlandish tales. He thought he would write a book about these guys sometime. Despite all the differences in these men, Tommy knew that in a tight, they would have each other's backs. They were, after all, "Marine Raiders." The best of the best.

~2~

The Beach

At 1800 hours, word came that they should get all their gear organized. Tonight they would execute their first mission. They would be boarding a small landing craft that would take them to within a mile of the beach of this very small island that had no name. It was just a number on a map. From the landing craft they would board rafts and would hit the beach under cover of darkness. They would make a hit-and-run raid on an airstrip that had been cut out of the jungle at the base of a mountain. They were to destroy as many of the planes and the hangars as possible. The command post and radio station were also targeted.

Thirty Marine Raiders would land on the beach and split into three ten-man squads. Two squads would plant explosives on the planes and hangars. One squad would incapacitate the command post and radio station.

They had one hour and twenty minutes to plant their timed explosives. They were to be back on their rafts at 0410 hours.

Not a shot was fired that night. The Japs suspected nothing. There were only four guards on duty and they were not alert. The guards were dispatched silently with slit throats or piano wire around their necks.

The three squads finished their work and were on the beach at 0405 hours where they immediately shoved off and were about half a mile from the beach when the explosions started. Burning gasoline and oil make a very bright fire when exploded. It looked like the sun was rising. Tommy thought how fitting. Rising Sun ... like the Japanese flag.

Spirits were high when they boarded the troop ship. By 0800 hours they were eating their breakfast and were about twenty miles from the island. After breakfast, the men were debriefed one squad at a time.

That evening an observer plane sent word that only one plane had somehow escaped destruction. But it was grounded. Apparently they did not have enough gasoline left to fly it off the island.

The raiders were assembled and a young

captain accompanied by a Navy lieutenant came before them and commended their success. He said their action would be recorded in their personnel files.

They were told that they could tell no one about this mission. Tommy was disappointed. He wanted to write home about it. But letters were being censored. So when he wrote, he said it had been an uneventful couple of days. He put quotation marks around "uneventful," hoping his folks would read between the lines.

Tommy's squad was on a high from this successful mission. But the high wore off after a couple of weeks. They were ready for more action. He at least wanted to fire his BAR in battle.

The troop ship sailed to Pearl Harbor and offloaded the troops on May 7, 1942. Tommy and his outfit were housed in old barracks in the boondocks. A beer hall was set up in another old barn of a building. Tommy wasn't interested. He had never tasted beer and saw no need to start now. His mother would not have approved. So Tommy did what he had been doing——not much of anything.

To keep the troops occupied, they were sent on ten-mile hikes and fired their weapons every week.

They were in this camp for two months. Tommy was a little disgusted. The news from the Pacific was all bad news. The Philippines had fallen. General MacArthur had left Corregidor, saying, "I shall return."

Then on the sixth of July, Tommy and his unit of Marine Raiders were loaded on a small troop ship and sailed out of Pearl Harbor. No word of any kind, but something was up.

For almost a month, they sailed around what seemed to be in circles. Then on the second of August, Tommy's unit was unloaded over the side into a submarine. It was a tight fit. Some of the submarine personnel had been transferred to the troop ship to make room for the thirty Raiders. It was not too bad at night when they ran on the surface. The men took turns going up on the deck for fresh air. Daylight hours were the worst when they mostly ran submerged. Fortunately, none of the Raiders were claustrophobic.

The second day at dawn while still on the surface, an alarm sounded and the sub began a fast dive towards the bottom of the Pacific. Everyone was ordered to be absolutely quiet. No talking, no moving about. A Japanese destroyer was almost overhead.

Soon, there was a loud explosion and the sub

shook violently. The lights flickered and a water pipe sprang a leak. Then there were several more explosions, and each time the sub shook. The crew of the sub didn't seem excited at all. This must have been routine to them. This pounding went on for almost an hour. Finally, the explosions seemed farther away and at last, an all-clear was given. There was a collective sigh of relief. The submarine's crew was a little perplexed that they were not allowed to follow the destroyer and take a shot at it. But they had a bigger mission, and that was to deliver these Raiders safely to a designated island.

On August 16th, the Raiders were called up on deck and told their mission. It was Makin Atoll in the Gilbert Islands. It was about midnight when the submarine Tommy and his unit were on met up with three other submarines with more Marine Raiders aboard each of them. One hundred twenty-two men in all.

The small rafts with outboard engines were loaded and launched at midnight. The seas were rough and plans were changed. They had intended to land on two different beaches. But Colonel Carson thought it best to all land on one beach.

They struck inland to engage the Japanese.

There was stiff resistance with two intense Banzai charges by the Japs. The .30 caliber machine guns and the men with the BARs were quite effective and in the end, most of the 160 Japanese on the island were killed. The garrison on the island was basically wiped out. However, there was a cost involved. Eighteen Raiders were killed and twelve were missing. Later, it was learned that the twelve missing were taken captive and executed by the commander on the island before he was killed.

Tommy's unit suffered two of those losses. As the unit was debriefed, it was found that Tommy and the machine gun crew had accounted for fifty-eight of the dead Japanese. This was on account of the Banzai charges in which they were mowed down like cutting wheat back on the farm. At one point, the Japanese bodies piled up in front of the machine gun, and one of the crew had to kick the bodies from in front as they were blocking the fire.

The mission could not be called a complete success as the dozen or so Japanese left on the island raised the "Rising Sun" flag the next morning within the walls of the garrison. Nor did the Raiders capture any prisoners, which would have provided valuable intelligence. The Japanese also became more alert in the future. However, it did show the

Japanese that the Americans could hit back hard.

Tommy began to think back on that Sunday when America suffered so many losses at Pearl Harbor. At that time, he only had a rather disconnected dislike for the Japanese. But after each of the two battles he had been in, his dislike had grown to rage and hatred for this enemy. It was personal to him as he had seen men with whom he had trained and eaten with, killed within arm's reach. He had heard the wounded calling for their mothers.

He thought it strange that when grown men were injured or near death, they always called for their mothers ... never heard one ever call for his dad. He had also heard men praying, the ones who had confessed before to not believing in God. Tommy was a believer. He couldn't understand a man praying to a God that he didn't believe existed.

Tommy had been close enough to the enemy to smell their sweat and their bad breath. Close enough to see their slanted eyes as they were fixed in death. But they didn't seem human. They seemed more like wild beasts to him.

War does horrible things to men, even men who believe in the sanctity of life. Tommy made a vow to himself. He would kill as many Japs as he could, any way he could. The innocent boy who had not even finished high school and could barely shave, had grown into a man almost overnight. Life was now so much different from his life on the farm. The boy who could once barely stand the yearly hog butchering was now excited about killing men.

Back to Pearl Harbor for rest and relaxation for two months. Then back aboard a troop ship.

Tommy marked days off the calendar one day at a time for thirty-one days. Finally, word came to get ready for another important assignment. Carson's Raiders were to hit a beach on an island, of which the name sounded like someone sneezed. Colonel Carson headed up his men personally. He gave his men a pep talk the night before. They also were invited to the aft deck for a religious service. The priest offered Mass, while the Methodist chaplain had a brief homily and offered a long, sincere prayer for the men and their families back home. The last thing they did before they lay down for the evening was a last-minute check of all their weapons and other equipment. They were pumped up and ready on November 2, 1942.

At 0430 hours, they began to board the landing

craft. It was a warm morning. The men were sweating like hogs. Some of the men were sick and vomiting. It was not so much from being seasick as from anticipation, fright, and nervousness. Say what you will, but God did not create young men to be thinking about killing, death, and mayhem. Tommy noticed several of the men praying, and he quickly bowed his head for a short prayer himself.

It was almost daylight when the ramp on the landing craft splashed to the floor of the beach in waist-deep water. The men began to scramble into the water. Bullets were hitting the water, and a few pinged off the side of the landing craft. Men began to shout and cry. A man within two feet of him just slid beneath the water without a sound except for the thud that had just hit him in the chest.

Tommy saw fire coming from the underbrush, which was about sixty yards from the edge of the water. There was no cover between the water and the underbrush. He noted that the sand on that beach was as white as snow. Colonel Carson was leading like a wild man. He yelled, "Come on, Raiders, charge the bastards!" With a man like that leading, there was nothing else to do except charge! Tommy quick fired his BAR by just holding the trigger. It fired automatically until the magazine was empty. He knelt long enough to put in another clip. This time, he fired one or two shots at a time at the smoke and flashes of fire from the underbrush.

The first twenty or so Raiders got to the line of fire with bayonets fixed, but the Japs had retreated inland several hundred yards. Colonel Carson, to Tommy's surprise, was unscathed. As the others reached the tree line, Colonel Carson quickly passed the word along to dig foxholes and set up the .30 caliber machine guns and mortars. He surmised the enemy was setting a trap for them as they had retreated so quickly. He would not follow them into the trap. In a couple of hours, heavier equipment had reached their positions. They now had enough firepower to handle most any attack.

At high noon, suddenly all hell broke loose. The Japs were throwing everything they had at them. They even had two tanks brought up into position. Now, Japanese tanks were not as large or foreboding as American M4 Sherman tanks. They were also lightly armored and easier to knock out.

A bazooka team knocked one of them out with one shot. The other tank retreated into the jungle. But in the meantime, it looked like a thousand men had appeared and were not only firing their weapons, they were advancing at a fast pace.

Actually, they were running toward the Raider line of defense, which was now dug in.

The Raiders began to fire as quickly as they could. The quick burp of the .45 caliber Tommy guns, along with the insistent racket of the .30 caliber machine guns. The sharper crack of the M1s, carbines, and Browning automatics. The distinct metallic clink as the mortar rounds were fed into the tubes of the mortars, and the dull thud as it left the tube. Then seconds later came the explosion of the shells as they hit the targets. The occasional clunk as a spent shell casing or clip striking a helmet as it was ejected from a weapon. Men were yelling for more ammo, crying for their mothers, or calling on Jesus. There is no more horrifying sound than the sound of battle.

Tommy lay as flat on the ground, making as small a target of his six-foot-four frame as possible. Bullets hit the ground and whistled above his head, miraculously missing him. He fired and fired but the yellow-skinned little men just kept coming. Colonel Carson passed the word along for Tommy with his BAR to get close to the .30 caliber machine gun and provide cover while they reloaded a belt into it. He lay next to the sandbagged machine gun nest. He had fired so many rounds so quickly that he couldn't touch the muzzle, and hoped it wouldn't warp.

A wave of a dozen or more smallish yellow men in brown uniforms were within twenty feet. The machine gun swept the field and mowed them down. They kept coming. A dozen or two dozen at a time. The bodies piled on top of each other. Tommy stopped firing long enough to push three or four bodies aside so the machine gun had a clear field of fire. Three more Raiders with fixed bayonets on their M1s appeared and took on three Japanese marines that had made it almost to the machine gun position. The Raiders made very quick work of them before jumping back down into the machine gun nest. Fortunately, the wave stopped coming.

A count was made of the casualties. There were twenty walking wounded (still able to fight.) A dozen wounded men had been carried to the beach for transportation to a ship. There were ten dead and three missing. The battle had lasted almost one hour. Tommy removed his helmet and found two dings in it——from bullets, he supposed. He didn't remember them hitting it. However, he was unscathed.

The enemy seemed to have just evaporated back into the jungle. The toll on the Japanese was much heavier. Over fifty bodies could be counted in the immediate vicinity of the machine gun. However, it was now very quiet. *Too quiet*, Tommy thought. He was right. Because as night began to fall and shadows grew long, the shadows also seemed to move. He thought it must be his imagination. But then a shot rang out and a marine fifty yards away was struck in the head and killed instantly. Snipers. There were snipers among the trees. The order came down. Stay in your foxhole and keep your helmet on. Try to sight the snipers, but don't fire on them until you are sure you have a clear shot.

A Marine corporal with a sniper rifle showed up just about the time it was too dark to see. He lay down beside Tommy with his eyes taking in the scene before him. He was specially trained in finding and shooting snipers or enemy officers. Tommy felt comforted to have him in the same foxhole, at least until he found out enemy snipers were trained the same way. Then he felt like he was lying next to a target.

At about 2100 hours, what sounded like an American voice called out, "Help me, Johnny, help me. Johnny, come get me ... I'm hurt ... I can't move ... please help me." The sniper next to Tommy said, "Stay put. That's a Jap."

The word was passed along that no one was to reply or show themselves. This was a common ploy used by the Japanese to lure men into the open. But it kept up all night long. Every few minutes an American-sounding voice calling a name and asking for help. The men were relieved that it was not a wounded comrade in trouble ... but it was still nerve-wracking. The Japanese were very good at playing mind games.

At 0700 hours, Sergeant Simpson called Tommy and three other men from Company C to go on a patrol. The main body of Japanese had seemed to just melt away into the jungle. There were still some snipers around. They were mostly in the tall palm trees. When one was spotted, the Raider sniper would knock him out of the tree. At least partway out of the tree. They had tied themselves to the tree and when shot, they were left dangling by a rope like some exotic fruit. Then someone would shoot them again. Just to make sure.

Tommy's patrol was headed up by Lieutenant Jamison from the command post and Corporal Johnson. Johnson took the point. Lieutenant Jamison was next, followed by Tommy, and Private McCoy brought up the rear. Lieutenant Jamison had removed his insignia so as not to be a special target for some sniper.

They had traveled just about a mile and a half when they heard voices—Japs. They quickly got off the narrow trail into the underbrush. Two Japanese regular army soldiers walked by as if they were on a morning stroll. Lieutenant Jamison signaled that they should try to take them prisoners. Corporal Johnson grabbed the one next to him, putting his hand over his mouth and nose. The other soldier turned with a look of surprise and terror in his eyes, and brought his rifle to his waist as if to fire. Tommy rushed him and stuck his stiletto under his rib cage while knocking the rifle to the ground. He twisted the knife and plunged it in and out of the soldier's midsection several more times. Fortunately, no shot was fired.

Tommy made sure the Jap was dead before he let him drop to the ground. His mouth was dry, his palms sweaty, and his heart felt like it would beat out of his chest. Tommy knew he had killed others before ... but it was nothing like this. Up close and personal, with his own hands. Tommy wiped the blood off his stiletto on the blouse of the dead soldier before returning it to the sheath strapped to his thigh. He knelt beside the still body and looked into those dark, dead eyes as he patted the soldier's pockets. His cold eyes stared back as if mocking him. It was a snapshot that Tommy would never be fully able to erase from his mind.

He quickly collected a billfold, some odd-looking coins, a pocket watch, and a cigarette lighter. He left a pack of cigarettes, but took the soldier's weapon. Before he turned away, Tommy studied the dead soldier's face one last time. He looked to be no more than a teenager. Tommy thought perhaps he was reserve army or a new recruit, since he had not been very alert.

After a thorough search, the remaining prisoner was made to undress to his skivvies. He was marched with his hands on his head back down the trail toward the American lines. He might provide some valuable intelligence for the Americans. The prisoner, along with the weapons and his personal effects, was sent to the command post, which was still on the beach.

Tommy kept the dead soldier's billfold, coins, and pocket watch. Before he had time to rest, Tommy and the rest of the patrol were called to the command_post for debriefing. While there, he gave up the Japanese cigarette lighter. Colonel Carson commended all of the men for their performance and said it would be noted in their personnel record. Tommy heard no more from the prisoner.

But he couldn't get his mind off of the young, dead soldier.

That night just before dark while sitting in his foxhole, Tommy took out the contraband he had taken. He examined each item carefully. He wondered how the man had obtained each of these pieces and what they had meant to him. The pocket watch contained a picture of a young lady on the inside cover. She looked to be no more than twenty years old. There was what appeared to be a letter in the billfold with the strange Japanese markings written on both sides of very thin paper. He thought he would have it interpreted one day, if he were fortunate enough to make it home.

As he looked at these spoils of war, Tommy suddenly saw those dead eyes before him and had a horrible twinge of remorse. He began to weep as he did something he had not done in quite a while. He spoke to God in a short, sincere prayer. "God, you know I was not raised to hate, kill, or steal. Please, Lord, forgive me, and Lord, I just pray that this man's family will somehow be comforted." But to himself, he vowed to keep this evil deed locked in his heart and mind. His own family should never know.

This was the beginning of a condition which has

puzzled doctors for centuries. It has only recently been given a name. PTSD. Post Traumatic Symptom Disorder. All Tommy knew was he must never let anyone outside the circle of his comrades know what happened on that Jungle trail.

Tommy justified his action in his mind by saying he was just doing a job for which he had been trained. His dad had always told him, "If a job is worth doing, it's worth doing it right."

Tommy tried unsuccessfully to make peace with God. He did *temporarily* relegate it to a dark corner of his mind. To himself, he said, "*I have a war to fight and win, in order to get back to a normal world.*" Little did he know at the time, he would relive that moment over and over in horrible flashbacks and terrifying nightmares.

After several more days of fierce fighting, the Japanese resistance became weak with the exception of a few well-hidden snipers. Word came one evening that the Marine Raiders were being replaced by regular Army to finish mopping up and holding the island.

By noon the next day, Tommy was climbing aboard a troop transport ship. Two days later, they met a hospital ship and offloaded a few dozen wounded to be transported to Pearl Harbor.

There would be little rest for Carson's Raiders. A week later they were awakened at 0200 hours by the booming guns of nearby battleships. They were shelling another island upon which they would soon be landing.

The shelling of the island went on unceasingly until 0630 hours. The Raiders then went over the side into a landing craft and began the two-mile ride toward the island. It was just as before with some Raiders being sick and others telling silly stories to take their mind off of what was coming next.

At 0725, Tommy looked at his watch. Just then the ramp fell into very shallow water and they charged across the sandy white beach.

As they reached the tree line, all hell broke loose. The firing was from the underbrush no more than twenty yards away. They were ordered to get down and start firing. There was no visible target. Just smoke and muzzle flashes. The machine guns were set up quickly behind a fallen palm tree. Fortunately, some of the battleship shells had left large craters. So they did have foxholes already available. They just needed to dig them a little deeper when they had time.

Finally, when the mortars were in place and firing, the Jap firing stopped. Looking around,

Tommy spotted several bodies at the edge of the jungle. He quickly counted eleven Raiders lying still, as medics moved among them. Most were tagged as dead by placing their rifle with bayonet affixed barrel down in the sand beside them. Three were placed on stretchers and carried swiftly back toward the water.

A scouting patrol went into the jungle and returned a couple of hours later. They said the Japs had retreated five miles inland, leaving only a few stragglers. They had also brought with them three wounded Japanese regular army soldiers. After interrogation, it was believed this island was being set up as a staging area. It looked as though an airstrip was being cut out of the jungle.

Colonel Carson sent word that they would be moving inland in the morning after another patrol was sent out.

By 0900 hours the next morning, they were traveling inland, following the trail of the retreating Japs. As they approached a tall cliff-like hill, they began to take fire from the caverns in the cliff. Four 105 mm artillery pieces were brought close enough to fire directly into the cliff openings. The artillery guys were really good. Within half an hour there was no more firing from the caverns.

On the trail again, they came to a wide creek. As the first six or eight men entered the knee-deep water, they received fire. Two looked to have died instantly. The others made it back to the bank. Tommy's unit covered them. Suddenly, it looked as if there were hundreds of men dressed in brown uniforms with fixed bayonets on their rifles coming across the creek. They were shouting and blowing whistles.

Not only were they firing their rifles, some paused and threw grenades. The machine gun had been set up and Tommy was covering the nest with his BAR. The muddy creek had been turned to a tinge of rusty crimson with blood and gore. The machine gun kept a steady racket as it swept back and forth with bursts of fire at the charging mad men. Many brown-clad bodies were floating in grotesque, unnatural positions.

One wave of Japs almost reached the Raider line when Tommy realized he was down to his last two clips for his weapon. He heaved a grenade the ten short yards into the middle of this wave. It was devastating and halted the advance temporarily. He pulled the pins and tossed two more in quick succession before the charging wave could recover. At the same time, he was calling for more ammo. A young private that had just joined the unit pushed a belt with several pouches of ammo toward him for his BAR. Tommy also looked for some more grenades. There was a box of grenades in the machine gun nest. The ammo carrier in the nest tossed Tommy four grenades. He laid them out beside him on the ground just in case.

Tommy could hear the plunk and the thud as a Raider mortar was lobbing rounds beyond the creek. After several explosions, the firing from across the creek ceased.

The wounded and dead were carried to the rear as soon as possible. It was bad for the moral to leave them close by. In a couple of hours, a Navy chaplain moved among the men, New Testament in hand, asking if they needed anything. From time to time, he would pause and word a short prayer with a couple of men. He was an older man with gray hair and a disarming smile. *He is much too old to be on the battlefield.* However, his peaceful composure had a soothing effect on the men.

I think I'd like to hear him preach sometime, Tommy thought. He never got the chance, however. The next day, word came down that the quiet Navy chaplain had been killed by a sniper as he made his rounds. Tommy was so mad it made his blood boil.

It made no sense, killing a man who didn't even carry a weapon. He was learning that war makes no sense and is not fair.

Tommy awoke in his foxhole thinking of the men with whom he had trained. Several of these men were dead, or wounded so badly they had been evacuated to a hospital ship. Why was he still alive? He had feelings of guilt that he was unscathed. Then he remembered something his mother had said many times, "If we arise in the morning, God still has something for us to do." He thought, *Yes, I have Japs to kill.*

His thoughts were interrupted by the report of a sniper's rifle. A volley of several more shots rang out and a sniper was left dangling on the end of a rope not more than a hundred yards away. Immediately, the sniper's body was riddled by more angry fire. The authoritative voice of some sergeant shouted, "Cease fire!" Word filtered down that ammunition was to not be wasted on dead Japs, by order of the company commander.

Two days later, the order came that the Marine Raiders would be replaced by an Army reserve unit fresh from the States to finish mopping up this island. The Raiders would be going aboard a troop ship to an undisclosed destination. *That seems to be the standard operating procedure,* Tommy thought. *We never get to enjoy the satisfaction of finishing what we start.*

The ship they boarded was a large vessel which transported several thousand troops, both Marine and Army infantry units. The Raider officers were not too pleased about this, because as they said, a larger ship only meant a larger target for Japanese submarines. Besides this, being confined in close quarters on a ship was not good for the moral of the troops. There was more than normal grumbling, and a few fights broke out over card and dice games. However, no one got thrown in the brig, because they needed every available man to fight Japs.

Tommy tried to occupy himself with writing letters, reading old magazines and newspapers which were several weeks old. Every few days, a supply ship brought and picked up mail. Each evening, the ship's captain broadcast a radio program from Japan, with a sexy-sounding woman disk jockey, whom the men called "Tokyo Rose." She played all the latest popular American music and gave the weather report in Tokyo. Little did she know that these weather reports helped the Americans who were by now bombing Japanese cities with fire bombs. So the Americans knew what the weather was supposed to be in Japan. Rose spoke perfect English and spewed propaganda about how the Japanese were winning the war. The captain played this program for about half an hour each evening. The propaganda didn't work on the Americans. They loved the music while making jokes about "Rose."

The letters from home were always nice to read. Some of the men exchanged letters, if they were not too personal. The married men would read aloud the parts of the letters they thought others would enjoy, while keeping the very personal stuff to themselves. Occasionally, a man would get a "Dear John" letter and the other guys would have to spend a lot of time consoling him and convincing him that she was not worth the grief. There were much better women out there than that "fickle bitch."

Tommy's mother always wrote the letters from home to him. However, she would tell him what his dad and the other family members were doing and what they had to say. He could tell his dad was not getting the work out of the other kids that he had gotten out of him. So when Tommy wrote, he always told the kids to pitch in and help their daddy. He assured his mom that he was fine. His letters home got a little monotonous and repetitive, as he could not get specific about anything. The censurers would black out things they felt would give away anything harmful to the war effort. There were posters all over the ship reading, “Loose lips sink ships.” Tommy hoped everyone was as careful in their letters to home as he was.

~3~

One More Island

A rumor was passed along by word of mouth that they would be landing on another island very soon. At 1900 hours on February 15, 1943, the official-sounding voice on the ship's loudspeaker boomed out, "Now hear this ... Now hear this! All Marine personnel, begin loading the landing crafts by 0130 hours." The anticipated hour was quickly approaching. They now had a little over six hours to nervously await boarding.

Tommy always found that waiting was the worst. One never knew what was lurking just beyond those white Pacific beaches bordered by lush green vegetation. How could something that looked so beautifully peaceful conceal such devastation?

The men checked their weapons and other

equipment more than once as they waited for word to board what would be the last boat ride for many of these young warriors.

"Mount up!" came the cry from Sergeant Adams, which was echoed by dozens of other squad leaders on deck.

Dozens of helmeted, shadowy figures shuffled toward the rail and then down the cargo netting, which had been lowered over the side. Not an easy task in the daytime, but at night in an ocean with three- to five-foot swells, it was a challenge. Occasional cursing could be heard, and a thud as someone slipped and actually fell into the landing craft. However, a worse sound would have been someone falling into the water. Weighted down with backpack, ammo, and a weapon, a man would sink like a rock to the bottom, which was said to be about three hundred feet straight down.

The landing craft deck came up on a rising three-foot swell and met Tommy's feet on the way down. He immediately let go and was standing precariously on the deck. He swayed slightly and steadied himself by leaning against the side. Tommy, at six foot four, could just see over the side, but he was sure the shorter guys couldn't. However, it made no difference; there was still nothing but blackness. The landing craft circled in the water for what seemed like an hour until all the vessels were loaded with nervous, scared, sweaty men. The last vessel to hit the beach would only be ten minutes behind the first. It was essential that they all arrived one right behind the other in case the enemy put up a stiff fight.

Most of the men had been through this drill before, but the previous experiences didn't take the edge off. The engine on the landing craft roared as the throttle was thrust forward at top speed toward the beach. The pilot had been instructed to go full speed ahead in order to drive the vessel as far onto the beach as possible.

The landing craft scraped the bottom and slowed some, but then the engine revved up as the prop rose out of the water on a wave. As fortune would have it, that same wave lifted the craft and drove it toward the beach at a great rate of speed. After a few more seconds, it ground to a sudden stop and the ramp dropped with a loud splash into shallow water. The beach was quite visible now, as there was a large, full moon just rising in the east. Looking at the luminous dial of his watch, Tommy saw that it was 0345 hours. The timing had been perfect. Tommy also noted that fortunately, this beach was not as wide as the one on the last island.

The Raiders received some small weapons fire and what sounded like a few incoming mortar rounds. But they were able to advance to the first line of trees without casualties. The Japanese had been here. But they had abandoned their foxholes, which were mostly fortified with sand bags. What seemed strange was that the Japs had not put up a fight on this beach. Tommy thought something was not right.

There was also some equipment and personal effects lying around. The order was passed quickly to not touch any articles left by the Japs. They could be booby-trapped. This was found to be correct. Unfortunately, one Raider had not gotten the memo and was killed when he picked up a sword with a grenade buried beneath it. Great care was taken to defuse and clear these areas.

The Raiders' job was to advance as quickly as possible and engage the enemy. The Army infantry would be following them to do as usual–the mopping up and getting their faces in all the newsreels.

That afternoon, the Marines moved inland at a fast pace. The jungle got thicker, but the Japs had left a trail that a blind man could follow. They came to a wide creek at the foot of a mountain. After crossing it, they began to take fierce fire. Not just small arms, but mortars and artillery. Then the worst part—enemy fire from the rear. They were pinned down. Only one thing to do. They had to fight their way out of this one. Half of the troops were to advance as quickly as possible while the other half began to fire on the Japs who had attacked from the rear. There were not as many of the enemy behind them, but they were well-hidden and obviously had been trained in jungle fighting.

Tommy's squad had been ordered to fight the enemy that was attacking from the rear. They stayed down and crept forward slowly. Night was coming on, and in the dark, the enemy would have no special advantage. They were now happy that they had received such great training in night fighting.

When it was fully dark, Tommy's squad split into teams of two. Each man had a little toy cricket with which to signal each other. The toy cricket made a clicking sound when pressed. If they detected someone not far from them, they signaled. If there was no return signal, they fired.

There was sporadic fire all night. By daybreak, they estimated that they were about two miles from the creek and there was now no resistance. As they made their way back to their own line at the creek, they came across several dead Japanese soldiers. The strategy had worked very well. Tommy's squad joined the main force at the creek.

At about 0930 hours, a wave of Japanese came screaming and blowing whistles. They had fixed bayonets on their rifles. The Raiders laid down a deadly fire from two .30 caliber machine guns, two mortar teams, and fifty or so small arms. It was just like it had been in the other battles. The Japanese were mowed down like wheat at harvest time. They had no regard for their lives.

Finally, one wave of Japs got close enough to throw grenades. Suddenly, there was a blast behind Tommy, and he felt a horrible burning in the back of his shoulder and his butt. The breath had been knocked out of him. He could barely breathe. He felt like he was drowning and burning at the same time. He was sick to his stomach but nothing came up. He was sweating like he had never sweated even when he was putting up hay back home. Home? He was thinking of his mother and all his siblings standing beside her. Now he understood why so many men always called on their mothers as they lay dying. Tommy thought, *I must be dying.*

Tommy learned later that a Japanese grenade

had been tossed behind him and had showered him with shrapnel. A large piece had hit the back of his shoulder and smaller pieces had penetrated his butt. They felt like half a dozen bee stings. He had never realized that shrapnel would be so hot. The concussion had actually knocked the breath out of him. He was unable to move his right arm. The pain in it felt like when one strikes the crazy bone in their elbow and can't move it for a while. Only, this pain and paralysis didn't go away.

Rolling on his side and looking up, he saw Colonel Carson kneeling over him. Tommy saw his lips moving but there was just a buzz in his ears. Then he realized the Colonel was calling for a medic. He had his .45 caliber pistol in his hand and as a medic arrived, the Colonel stood, gave Tommy a thumbs-up, turned and shouted, "Come on, Raiders! Fix bayonets! Let's charge the bastards!" The medic arrived just then and poured sulfa powder directly into Tommy's shoulder wound and injected him with morphine. The pain was excruciating. But his hearing was returning. He heard the medic laugh and say, "The wounds in your ass are too far from your heart to kill you." After packing the huge hole in his shoulder with gauze, the medic said, "Buddy, you have a million dollar wound; you're state bound." The morphine took hold and that was the last thing Tommy remembered until he woke up on a hospital ship.

Tommy learned he was going to have to lie on his stomach for a while. It was embarrassing for him, as nurses not much older than him dressed the wounds on his "buttocks" as they called it. But they were very good at their craft, and within a few days he could roll over on his left side.

The other wounded men were cruder and kidded him about being shot in the "ass." Smiling, he thought of his mother. *She would bawl those guys out. She doesn't approve of such language.*

The doctors aboard the ship only packed and dressed the shoulder wound. It would have to wait until they got to Pearl Harbor to do the needed surgery. The hole in his shoulder was so large, one could lay a baseball in it.

Tommy felt so fortunate, however. Looking around one day, he saw men who were missing legs, arms, and eyes. Some of these men were bitter while others were just thankful to be alive. Tommy had a come-to-Jesus meeting late one night and thanked God for keeping him alive. He just prayed that he would be able to help his dad on the farm again.

At the hospital in Pearl Harbor, Tommy got all the TLC he needed. The hospital was as modern as any in the States he had seen. The surgeons were the best in the medical field.

He went through three surgeries in three days on his shoulder. They also dug more Japanese "souvenirs," as they called this shrapnel, out of his "ass." The surgeons were not as proper in their language as the nurses.

The food was really good at this hospital in Pearl Harbor. He had lost weight during the fighting. But now he was packing on a few pounds.

Since he couldn't use his right arm, a volunteer came to assist him. She was a young Hawaiian girl by the name of Jauna. She came and wrote letters for him, which he dictated. Jauna was cute as a "spotted pup," a favorite expression of his. When he told her to put that in his letter home, she giggled and blushed, but wrote it down.

Jauna came to visit him even when he didn't have a letter to dictate. Her daddy owned a pineapple plantation on the island. She told Tommy when he got well enough, she would show him around the plantation. But that never happened.

Some big brass came to the hospital two weeks after Tommy arrived at Pearl Harbor. It was some colonel along with a lieutenant and a sergeant. They had some medals they wanted to pin on some of the men in the ward. All got Purple Hearts, and some got other medals for valor. Tommy received two medals beside the Purple Heart.

One day about a month after he had arrived in Pearl Harbor, a tall, familiar figure walked through the door of Tommy's ward. It was Uncle Johnny. Johnny was in the Army Signal Corps. He was stationed at Pearl Harbor. This is as close to any fighting that he ever got. They had a great visit and ate lunch together out in the courtyard of the hospital.

After two months in the hospital and a month of rehab to get the motion back in his right arm, Tommy was sent back to the States. He had been promoted to corporal and was still needed in the service of his country. After a short two weeks at home, he was sent to Parris Island to assist in small arms training. It was an easy job, as about all he had to do was follow a sergeant around and echo what he had to say. He kind of laughed at himself. He hoped he was not acting like that bantam rooster, Corporal Jackson, whom he disliked when he was in basic training.

After a few weeks, Captain Hollingsworth called Tommy in and said he had another job for him. He was to be his driver. It was an even easier job. He drove the Jeep wherever Captain Hollingsworth needed to go. At other times, he answered the phone for Sergeant Cooper when he was busy typing up reports.

Tommy got a five-day pass and made a quick trip to Indiana. He had caught a ride with a man who said he was driving straight through to Camp Atterbury near Indianapolis. He called his family from a phone booth when they stopped for gas. Ruth said they would meet him at the gate of Camp Atterbury. It was less than a two-hour drive from Frankfort to Atterbury. Tommy did not have to wait. His dad and mother were waiting at the gate when Tommy and his driver drove up. Tommy's dad offered to pay the man for the ride. The man said, "No sir, it is I who owe your son for his service."

Back at the farm that evening, Ruth Neal cried when she saw her son's shoulder wound. Her beautiful son would bear that scar the rest of his life. But then she hugged him and thanked God he was alive. After this short visit, it was time to travel back to his base.

Thomas took Tommy as far as Indianapolis. He had used all his gas ration stamps and that was as far as he could take him. But Tommy caught a ride with a man who was going to Cincinnati. And he had no problem catching rides the rest of the way to Parris Island. Soldiers could always thumb a ride during the war.

On January 10, 1944, Tommy was sitting in the orderly room reading the paper and answering the telephone while Sergeant Cooper was typing. The phone rang. A major was on the line with an urgent call for Captain Hollingsworth. Tommy buzzed the captain. In about five minutes, Captain Hollingsworth came to the door and motioned for Tommy to come into his office. He had a serious look on his face. Tommy entered the office, stood at attention, and saluted. Captain Hollingsworth told him to be at ease and to sit down.

Tommy was being called back to active duty with his Raider unit. He would first have to be cleared by the camp doctor. This news came as a shock to Tommy, but in his heart he was happy. He had been feeling like he had abandoned his buddies since he had gotten to feel better. With the physical complete, the doctor signed off on his fitness for active duty. Tommy packed his duffel bag, and was issued a lighter-weight weapon at the order of the camp doctor. It was an M1 carbine. The carbine didn't pack the stopping power of a BAR or the Garand. However, it didn't kick one's shoulder as bad as the other two and with its short barrel, was a good jungle rifle.

The next day, Tommy was aboard an Army transport plane headed to California. Within a week, Tommy was at Pearl Harbor once more. And a week later was on some godforsaken island. As he walked down the gangplank to the dock below, he saw Lieutenant Dickerson sitting in a Jeep. But now the lieutenant was wearing captain's bars. As Tommy threw his duffel bag in the back and jumped in himself, he congratulated Captain Dickerson on his promotion.

At the squad tent where Tommy was dropped, a gang of Marine Raiders mobbed him and pounded him soundly on the back. One of them patted him on the butt as he asked, "How's your ass?" Tommy pretended to wince, and everyone howled with laughter. *Wow, it is good to be back.*

Tommy wondered how long they had been on

this island. They said ever since the battle in which Tommy had been wounded. They had taken that island and even got to mop up.

The American forces had been hopping islands and skipping over some. The Navy was keeping supplies from reaching some of the Japanese-occupied islands.

The rumor was that the big push would come when they actually had to invade Japan. Everyone knew that would be a blood bath. The Japs were fanatical. They didn't think like Americans. As one man said, "It's as if they didn't mind dying for the emperor." There was nervous laughter as one man said, "Well, I don't mind killing them, if they don't mind dying." They all realized invading Japan would be one tough job.

Late in January 1945, a rough-talking sergeant stuck his head in the tent and shouted, "Mount up, you bastards! We're loading ship." Once aboard ship, they were told their destination. They were headed for an island called Iwo Jima. "Never heard of it," one man said. "Me neither," piped up about half a dozen others. That was soon to change and would become household words in the States.

On February 19, 1945, a large force of marines

landed on the island of Iwo Jima. This was not an operation just for the Raiders. It was a huge operation called "Operation Detachment." Iwo, as it was called, had three well-fortified airfields. These airfields were surrounded by hills with gun emplacement in them. The entire island had to be captured, and it would not be easy.

Iwo was the last step on the way to Japan. At least, that's what they thought.

There was no doubt about the outcome. The American forces would prevail. But at what cost? The Navy, Marines, Army, and Army Air Corps were all involved in this battle. The Japanese army was cut off from their supplies and the air was commanded by American planes. The Japs must surrender or die.

For once, Tommy's unit was not the first to hit the beach. They were about the fourth wave of landing craft to come ashore. They came in right behind a column of those amazing Sherman tanks. Tommy thought it was kind of nice to be protected by those monsters. They were large, well-armored, and could lay down great fire power.

Carson's Raiders would be acting as support troops in case they were needed. They were needed on the second day. The island was fortified with heavy artillery and mortars. The only weakness of the Japanese was that they did not have enough ammunition or food for a long drawn-out campaign. And there was no way to get more supplies in.

The tanks were called up to begin shelling the gun emplacements in the hills. The Raiders were to stay with the tanks. Whenever the enemy showed itself, fire was concentrated on that area.

The one thing different was that the Japanese did not charge in waves as before. The Japanese could not afford to sacrifice any troops. However, the snipers were still ever present. But this time, they were not in trees, because there were very few trees on Iwo Jima. The Japanese snipers were in shallow holes in the earth with camouflaged trap doors. They would raise the trap doors a few inches and fire, usually at very close range. The Americans had stepped up their own sniper program. Whenever any Japanese officers were observed strutting about waving their sabers, a sniper would take him out. Every time a Jap sniper would fire, he was silenced quickly with either mortar rounds or intense small arms fire into the general area.

There was also a fairly new weapon in the American arsenal. It was a flame thrower. It worked like this: a mix of gasoline and diesel fuel in a pressurized tank was propelled out of the tank and ignited, throwing a stream of the flaming fuel into pill boxes or into the holes of the Japanese. Pretty scary stuff. Tommy saw many a Jap run from his hole on fire. Sometimes the marines would shoot the poor bastard to put him out of his misery. At other times they would just let them burn.

The fighting was fierce and intense as the main force pushed inland and began to surround and take the airfields one by one. Tommy's unit, however, was recalled to the rear and was responsible for protecting the command post. Squad tents were set up and it didn't seem much different than the camp on Pearl Harbor. They had better food than ever before, and were sleeping on cots instead of in foxholes. They listened to the broadcasts from Pearl Harbor and from Rose over in Tokyo. That first day back, when Tokyo Rose came on, Tommy thought, *Oh my God, is she still on?*

Tokyo Rose was indeed still very active with her propaganda. She tried to convince the Americans on Iwo Jima that they would be pushed into the sea. But she still played really good, big band music. It was also becoming more evident that the Japanese still had spies all over America.

One evening as Rose was broadcasting, she said the Americans were so desperate that they were now calling badly-wounded soldiers back into battle. Then she broadcast a name that made Tommy sit up and swing his feet off his cot. She said, "Corporal Thomas Neal, a Marine Raider who was badly wounded on February 18, 1943, has been called back into action to sacrifice his life in a lost cause on Iwo Jima." Tommy was shocked. He remembered the signs: *Loose Lips Sink Ships.* Someone had very loose lips. He was also very angry that she would use him for her propaganda. Through clinched teeth, he growled, "I'd like to get my hands on that slant-eyed Jap bitch."

On February 23rd, word came to headquarters that the highest point on Iwo Jima, Mount Suribachi, had been taken and the American flag planted right on top. It was a psychological victory. The news team which was on the island said they had pictures of it. They would like to see how Tokyo Rose would spin this. She never mentioned it.

On March 26th, a memo of congratulations for a job well done was sent to the troops. The battle for Iwo Jima was over. However, Tommy and his unit stayed on Iwo for another month.

After they returned to Pearl Harbor, the

Raiders trained for an invasion of Japan. Different scenarios were introduced into the training. Up to this point it had been jungle fighting for the Raiders. House-to-house fighting is much different and even more challenging. Simulated Japanese houses were set up. The men were told they needed to be prepared physically and mentally to kill women and children. It would not just be soldiers that would be trying to kill them.

One can only train so much before it gets boring. When one gets bored, one gets careless. The Raiders were ready to invade Japan and get it over with.

On May 7, 1945, the music on the radio in Tommie's squad tent was suddenly interrupted. The excited voice said, "Germany has surrendered to the Allied forces. The war in Europe is over." Whooping and hollering was heard all over the camp. But the celebration didn't last long. Japan still stood in the way of everyone going home.

Three months to the day, another very excited voice interrupted the music playing on the radio, and the monotony in the camp at Pearl Harbor. "A very powerful bomb was dropped on the city of

Hiroshima, Japan yesterday." The voice went on to say the city was utterly destroyed. Thousands upon thousands were killed. Strangely, there was only a brief moment of jubilation. For there was still no word about surrender.

Word came a few days later that a second bomb like the first had been dropped on another large city in Japan. Nagasaki was the target this time. Again, thousands died. These bombs were called "atomic bombs."

On August 15th, on the six o'clock news, the announcer said, "Japan has agreed to surrender." A huge shout went up in the camp. But no word came just yet as to when the men would be mustered out to go home. Everyone listened more intently to the radio broadcasts after this.

At noon on September 2, 1945, all personnel were listening to General MacArthur aboard the USS *Missouri*, which was anchored in Tokyo Bay, as he accepted the surrender of Japan. It was a recorded broadcast of this historic event, which officially ended WWII. At the end of the broadcast, a huge celebration started and didn't end for several hours.

~4~

Homeward Bound

A week later, Tommy received his orders. He, along with all of his unit, were being disbanded and discharged. However, anyone wanting to re-up in the Marines could do so. Needless to say, no line formed for reenlistments. With his honorable discharge securely buttoned in his shirt pocket, Tommy boarded a ship headed to San Diego, California. From there, he took a train to Indianapolis. This was a trip which took four days, as there were many stops along the way.

At home, Tommy had a hard time falling asleep at night. And when he slept, he suddenly awoke in a sweat. Sometimes he imagined it was the blast of a grenade that brought him awake. He had tremendous anxiety attacks. Besides this, as the cold damp weather of an Indiana fall came on, his shoulder hurt much worse.

At the Veterans Hospital in Indianapolis, x-rays showed there was still some metal in his shoulder. More surgeries were in order. As for his anxiety, it was recommended he keep busy, and he was prescribed some pills.

That fall, he helped with the corn harvest and the hog killing that all the farmers did every year. There would be hams, sausage, and sides of bacon in the smokehouse. When it came to the actual killing, Tommy declined the offer to shoot the hog. He had his belly full of killing. Tommy didn't even go rabbit hunting with the men on Thanksgiving, as had been his custom. He told them that he had been "the rabbit" and it was not fun.

Other than this, life on the farm was just about like it was when he left. That first Sunday back, Tommy awakened early and lay staring at the ceiling. He heard his dad stoking the cook stove in the kitchen. He started to pull on his well-worn blue jeans and then realized it was Sunday. For the first time since he was about ten years old, he really didn't want to go to church. It wasn't that he didn't love God. But crowds bothered him. He also knew there would be a lot of questions that he didn't want to answer.

But to keep his mom happy, he would go to church with the family. He took a bird bath in cold water and even shaved with the cold water. He put on a white shirt, a green and yellow striped tie, and the only sports coat he owned, which was a tad too small. His pants were also really tight around the waist, but he squeezed into them. Looking in the mirror as he slicked down his hair, which was beginning to grow long again, he thought, *There. That should make Mom happy.* Everyone was excited at breakfast; their family hero was going to church with them.

The ride to church was hilarious as all the kids had grown. They were packed like sardines in that Chevy. As they parked and began to exit the car, Tommy laughed to himself. *We must look like a bunch of clowns getting out of one of those funny little cars at a circus.*

There was a lot of really good fellowship before and after the services. The worship time itself was a little boring. The preacher was an old man who had come out of retirement to fill in during the war. His sermon was as dry as powder. One of the elders announced that Jake Jennings would be back in the pulpit the next Sunday. He had just been discharged from the paratroopers. Word was that he had been wounded in Italy not long before the Germans surrendered. Tommy thought, *We will have something in common.*

On Wednesday of that week, Tommy purchased a well-used Ford Coupe off of a neighbor who had kept it stored in his barn during the war. It didn't look so hot but it was fast, as it had a V-8 under the hood. So the very next Sunday, the family went to church in two cars, with his brothers riding in the car with him.

Everyone was excited. Preacher Jake was supposed to preach this Sunday.

Most of the congregation was standing out in front of the building when Jake drove up. Jake still had his 1937 Plymouth, which he had bought before the war. He had drained the radiator and had put it up on blocks in a barn while he was serving his country.

Jake parked in his reserved parking space in front of one of the hitching posts. But he just sat in the car a couple of minutes with his head bowed. He finally opened the door and slowly exited. Reaching in, he retrieved something from the back seat. It was a pair of crutches. As he came around the car on the crutches, someone gave an audible gasp. Jake's left leg was missing. He paused and surveyed the people, and then the building. His eyes began to lift toward heaven with his gaze finally coming to rest on the steeple. He nodded his head as if approving of his surroundings. Then someone in back started slowly clapping and soon everyone was clapping for him. Jake was visibly moved, as was Tommy.

Tommy stood at attention with tears streaming down his face. Then he snapped a Marine Raider salute toward Jake that would have made his captain proud. Tommy held his salute for several seconds. Jake acknowledged Tommy with a smile and a short, curt salute back.

Within seconds, Jake was surrounded. People wanted to assist him. But Jake said, "I can handle this. I spent a month in rehab to learn how to do it." He deftly ascended the three steps into the church building like he had been doing it all his life. He had even learned how to hold his small Bible and a crutch at the same time.

It was an emotional service that day. Jake had greatly improved his knowledge as well as his delivery. At the very beginning of the service, Jake told the congregation that he would soon have a prosthesis. Then he said, "For you hillbillies, that's a peg leg." That broke the ice and everyone laughed.

Thank you, Lord, that I lost no limbs, Tommy thought. *My wounds are almost invisible ... almost.*

One day in late winter, Tommy noticed his dad was not moving as fast as he once did. He looked old and tired. He also noticed his dad clutching at his chest after shoveling feed into the hog feeder one day. But Thomas denied that anything was wrong. "Just a little indigestion," he said.

Tommy took his brothers aside and had a serious talk with them about helping their dad more. They looked up to Tommy and wanted to please him. Thomas Sr. was grateful to Tommy for giving the boys that pep talk.

Tommy always wanted to own a trucking business. He bought a used lime spreading truck and all that spring, he spread lime, nitrogen, and fertilizer. He made a nice profit that spring. Tommy was still living at home. Everyone liked it that way. He only went out on Saturday night to the movies and to a drive-in restaurant that had just opened in town.

There was a young carhop that always waited

on Tommy when he came to the drive-in. She was five years younger than Tommy. She had dark brown hair, big brown eyes and a nice figure. Her name was Sally Conner. Sally made Tommy feel good with her bubbly personality and her beautiful smile. One night as she was taking Tommy's order, out of the clear blue sky, he asked her if she would like to go to a movie with him some evening. She smiled and without any hesitation, said, "Sure would."

The next Sunday evening, they saw *Lassie Come Home* at the Avon. After the show, they walked across the street to the Sugar Bowl, which was a local burger and shake joint. Mostly, teenagers hung out there. But Tommy had missed some of his best teenage years.

This was the start of a relationship that lasted three years. But every time Sally wanted to get more serious, Tommy just couldn't take the next step. Finally, one Saturday evening Sally tearfully told Tommy she needed to move on with her life. That was the last he saw of her except from a distance. The war had produced one more casualty. This was perhaps one of the deepest wounds of all.

One evening in early spring, Tommy walked into

the kitchen and was washing his hands before supper, when his mother asked if his dad was coming in for supper. He looked at her with a surprised look on his face. Tommy said, “Mom, I just came in from spreading lime. Surely, Dad has come in and you didn’t see him.”

“No, I’m sure he hasn’t.”

Tommy got back in his jacket and headed to the barn. He called out, “Dad ... Dad?” as he entered the barn.

The cows were not in the barn. They were still standing in the tromp shed, waiting to be milked. A very sick feeling came over Tommy. He looked all over the barn and called for his dad. The only sound was of the cows lowing. He flipped the light switch, which turned on the light in the hay mow, and ascended the ladder. His dad lay face down, sprawled awkwardly, across a bale of hay. Tommy turned his dad on his side. His eyes were fixed in death. Tommy had seen this look too many times.

Three days later, Thomas Neal was laid to rest in the picturesque cemetery next to Bear Creek Church of Christ. His grave was surrounded by his family, the church members, and just about everyone in that part of the county. Mr. Tom, as he was called, was a very fortunate man to be loved by so many people.

Tommy called the family around the kitchen table that night after the dishes had been cleared. His mom had not cooked a meal for three days. These dishes would need to be returned to all the folks who had brought the food in. But this meeting was not about dishes.

Someone needed to take charge. It was decided Ruth would run the house and manage the finances. The three girls would help her with the housework, gardening, and taking care of the chickens. Tommy would manage the farm, with the help of his two brothers. There were no protests. The warrior had returned and it was now his turn to make sure the farm was a success and would stay in the family. Tommy even had plans in his mind to expand the farm.

Tommy kept his truck and when fall came, he got a bargain on another lime spreading truck. He hired two men who owned small farms to drive the trucks for him. It would supplement their incomes. Tommy also traded in his old car for an almost new Ford pickup truck with stock racks on the bed.

Tommy spent every waking minute planning,

supervising, and managing the farm and his small business. He was so tired at the end of the day that he simply ate, took a bath, and fell asleep as soon as his head hit the pillow.

He was up before daybreak every morning, making sure the boys were up and out doing their chores. The dairy business was good. He would add to the herd next year.

One day, late in 1949, Tommy had business in Indianapolis. He went into a restaurant for lunch. A young oriental girl waited on him. As she took his order, Tommy looked up from the menu and had a flashback. He was staring into a pocket watch at the face of a young Japanese girl. But the flashback was worse than that. He suddenly saw the lifeless face of a young Japanese soldier. It was the soldier he had killed with his stiletto.

Tommy pushed away from the table and walked out on the street. He was suddenly sick to his stomach and had broken out in a sweat. He climbed into his pickup truck, gripping the wheel so hard his knuckles were white. It began with a groan deep in his throat and suddenly he was sobbing so loud he was afraid someone would hear him. Tears streamed down his face. He found a mechanics rag in the glove box and wiped the wetness from his cheeks. Tommy told no one else about this. He must bear this cross alone.

At about 2:00 a.m., after a fitful night trying to sleep, Tommy crept into the attic and found his Marine foot locker. He had not opened it in years. He didn't remember what he had done with the key. With his pocket knife he jimmied the lock. Everything was just as he had left it. He was a little surprised the boys had not gotten into it. Good thing he had locked it.

Wrapped in a ragged U.S. Marines towel at the very bottom of the footlocker were the tangible memories of war. Lifting the treasures out one by one, Tommy laid them in the tray. There was a billfold containing the very thin paper with Japanese writing on both sides. He still supposed it was a letter. Then he examined the coins, turning them over in his palm. Next was the pocket watch. Almost unconsciously, he wound it and held it to his ear. It was ticking. He rubbed it softly with the towel in his fingers before gingerly opening the cover. There was that pretty young face looking back at him. He again had pangs of guilt which he had felt years before. He had to find out what the paper had written on it.

~5~

The Mystery Unfolds

He didn't think Indianapolis had any Japanese communities. The phone book gave no clues. Tommy called his former high school principal who, as he remembered, had also taught government and social studies. Perhaps he could tell him of a place to have the writing on the paper translated.

Dr. Paul Christian was the principal. Next morning on the phone, Tommy learned that he had recently retired. But he seemed genuinely happy to hear from a former student. Especially a "local hero," as he called Tommy. Tommy felt like anything but a hero at that moment. He explained what he wanted but didn't tell him why. Dr. Christian told him he had an idea and would give him a call the next day.

Down in Bloomington, at Indiana University

was a Japanese professor, who was a naturalized U.S. citizen. Dr. Christian had studied anthropology under this professor. Sadly, this professor had spent the war in an internment camp in California. However, he told Dr. Christian he would be more than happy to help this young man.

Dr. Katsu Ito opened his study door to Tommy and Dr. Christian on the next Friday afternoon. He was a short, slightly-built man who looked to be more than seventy years old. He greeted these two tall Americans with a smile and a polite bow from the waist. After introductions and some small talk, Tommy opened an old leather satchel that he had found in the attic. Reaching into it, he produced a worn, brown billfold with the paper still folded inside. Next, he brought out the pocket watch and coins. He laid them all carefully on Dr. Ito's desk.

Professor Ito asked if he could examine them.

"Yes sir, that's why I brought them to you."

Dr. Ito carefully examined all of these artifacts. He told how much each of the coins had been worth before the war. As he examined the watch, he said it was one of the finest watches that Japanese craftsmen could make. Then he gently unfolded the thin paper. He said it was called "rice paper," as it was made from rice instead of pulpwood.

He held the paper under a bright lamp and read one side to himself. Quietly turning the paper over, he read the other side. The professor tilted his head with interest, smiled, and said it was a letter from someone's father. The recipient was the man's soldier son. The writer mentioned a lady who had been selected as a wife for his son, and a second lady who was the boy's mother. The professor said the letter was dated July 10, 1942. It also had a return address on it. He noted that when it was folded a certain way it needed no envelope. That was the way it was sent to save on paper. He also said it was the fathers who usually wrote letters to their sons. The return address was from a small town called Bancho, less than two miles from Tokyo. The professor was familiar with this town as he once had family from there. However, he had not heard from them since before the war.

Just then, an older lady entered the study with a tray and she, too, bowed. She was serving these guests tea from the daintiest teacups Tommy had ever seen. Tommy usually didn't drink tea, but he didn't want to be impolite, so he drank the tea and found it to be very good.

Tommy asked the professor if he could actually transcribe word for word what the letter said. The professor nodded and motioned to the lady whom he had introduced as his secretary. He spoke to her in Japanese. She abruptly left after bowing, but was back within a couple of minutes. Dr. Ito took the fountain pen and paper she had laid on the desk before him and began to write. The others sat silently just watching as he wrote.

After about fifteen minutes, Professor Ito handed him the two papers and asked, "Are you able to decipher my penmanship?"

Tommy looked at the paper. It was the clearest, most beautiful handwriting Tommy had ever seen. "Oh my goodness, yes sir, I can certainly read this. Thank you so very much." Then as an afterthought, "What do I owe you for doing this for me?"

The old professor looked as if he was offended but graciously said, "You don't owe me anything, young man. I found this very fascinating. So, I thank you."

Tommy had one more question. "What do you think would be the chances of contacting someone in this family?"

The old professor thought a minute, shook his head, and said, "Little to none. You see, people have been displaced by the war, and many records have been destroyed." Tommy thanked the professor again before leaving.

Dr. Christian and Tommy rode back to Frankfort, each lost in their own very private thoughts. Tommy had never been interested in things of the past, but now he wanted to know everything he could about the dead soldier and the mysterious, pretty lady in the watch. But most of all, he wanted to beg forgiveness from this family.

Tommy's trip to Bloomington had only increased his curiosity. Dr. Christian helped him write to the U.S. Embassy in Japan. In a couple of weeks, Tommy received a letter from the embassy. The letter said they would try to help him locate this family, as they were trying to build a stronger, more trusting relationship with the Japanese people. It sounded encouraging.

Tommy had much work to do on the farm in order to keep the boys busy. He also had his two trucks to look after and maintain. He temporarily pushed the Japanese business aside. In mid-July, things slowed down on the farm. Tommy began to think again about the family in Japan. Just as he was about to write another letter, he received a very official-looking letter from Tokyo, Japan. He quickly opened the letter. A family by the name of

Sato had been found. The patriarch of this family, who was from the city of Bancho, said they had been notified that his grandson was killed on an island in the Pacific in November 1942. The grandson's name was Hiroto Sato.

Tommy suddenly had mixed emotions. It was good news, but at the same time he was as freighted as he had ever been in battle.

Two nights later, Tommy sat and wrote a letter to the Sato family. He addressed the letter to the patriarch whose name was Hibiki Sato. Tommy simply said he had some things which belonged to Hiroto Sato that he wanted to return to the family. He added that he wanted to personally present this property to them and would try to arrange to visit them as soon as possible.

Tommy had no idea how he was going to do this. All he knew was that he was going to do it.

On the next Sunday after church, Tommy asked Jake Jennings to go to lunch with him at the Sugar Bowl in town. At lunch, Tommy told Jake the whole story of killing the young Japanese soldier and all about the souvenirs he kept. Then he told Jake what he had in mind. Jake listened with a look of compassion on his face. When they were back in Tommy's truck, Jake had prayer for him. Then he said, “Tommy, I am going to help you get to Japan.” He continued, “But I want you to tell your story in church. I know you have asked God to forgive you and I am sure he has ... that is what God does best. But I believe when you tell your story to other Christians, you will feel so much better.” Tommy didn’t make any promises. He just said, “I’ll think about it.”

And think he did ... for the next two weeks. At the end of the service that second week, when the invitation was given, with tears in his eyes, Tommy walked to the front and took Jake’s hand. Jake hugged Tommy until the invitation song was finished.

Tommy turned to face the congregation and asked them to be seated. “I have a story to tell you.” Jake sat down on the front pew and gave him a thumbs-up. The floor belonged to Tommy.

With a very dry mouth and sweaty palms, Tommy poured out his story to a congregation that was held spellbound. He had to pause from time to time and compose himself. In closing, he told the congregation, “I must go and beg forgiveness from the Sato family.” Somewhere in the back there came a very audible “amen.” Some of the older ladies were dabbing at their eyes with their handkerchiefs.

Tommy retreated to his seat while Jake stood. This time he was a little unsteady on his artificial leg. He said, "I have a challenge to all of us." After a slight pause, he continued. "I want Bear Creek Church to provide the money for Tommy's trip to Japan." Heads were nodding in approval. Old Man Stanley Jackson, who never wanted to spend church money on anything, said loudly, "Amen, brother."

Later, with a smile on his face, Jake shook Tommy's hand at the door and whispered, "We witnessed a miracle today," as he nodded toward Brother Stanley Jackson.

Six weeks later, Jake presented Tommy with the money for his trip to Japan, from the good folks at Bear Creek Church.

The last time Tommy had been on a ship was when he was transported from Pearl Harbor to San Diego five years before. This time he boarded in San Francisco. Seven days later, he was standing at the rail as the ship steamed into Tokyo Bay. His heart was pounding furiously in his chest. He was excited but scared. He felt almost like he had just before hitting an island beach years before.

The State Department had worked with the War Department to make arrangements since the War Department still had oversight of the Japanese government. Tommy was to meet a representative who would transport him to the city of Bancho. The mayor of that city was to send an aide to meet with Tommy and his escort, to serve as his interpreter.

The mayor said they had located a Sato family that was more than likely the people whom he sought. They had lost a boy by the name of Hiroto Sato during the war.

Tommy spent that night in a small hotel in downtown Tokyo. He once more opened the worn, brown leather satchel in which his treasures had traveled.

He looked at them again and prayed they would find their way to the Sato family.

The next morning, Tommy and his escorts arrived in an open Jeep in front of a small, fragile-looking house on a side street. As they approached the front door, an older lady slid the door open and bowed. She held her bow for several seconds until the mayor's aide spoke to her. She said something to the aide and led them inside the house.

Just inside the door, the escorts began to take off their shoes, and Tommy followed their lead.

Tommy noticed there was no furniture except for a low table with pads spread around it.

Just then, a tall, thin man with grey hair came into the room. Some words were spoken by the aide and they all began to bow to each other. Tommy again followed suit as all eyes were now upon him.

The tall Japanese man was introduced as Hibiki Sato, the grandfather of Hioto. Tommy said he hoped he had found the right family. He reached into the satchel and brought out the pocket watch. He held it up by its rather delicate chain. All eyes were upon it ... then expressions changed. The lady who had opened the door spoke to Hibiki Sato and began to weep. Hibiki spoke, and the interpreter, said, "Yes, that belonged to his grandson."

Tommy spoke to the interpreter and explained that it was he who had killed Hioto on that Pacific island years before. He wanted this family to know that he was the one and that he had taken these personal effects. He wanted to return them and extend his sorrow. He also wanted very much to beg their forgiveness.

Tommy asked the interpreter if he could lay all these things on the low table in the room. After speaking to Hibiki, he turned and nodded. Tommy laid them all on the table. The coins and the watch, which he opened, were laid out first. Then, as he took out the billfold, he carefully unfolded the paper with the writing on both sides. The man and woman examined all of these things, speaking among themselves. The man examined the billfold, watch, and the paper.

He then turned and spoke to all of them. The mayor's aide said they should all be seated at the low table. After sitting on the padded floor at the table, the lady who Tommy learned was Aiko Sato, the mother of Hioto Sato, abruptly left the room.

The interpreter spoke at length with Hibiki Sato in the absence of Aiko. Hibiki's expression never changed, but he never took his eyes from Tommy.

The interpreter said he had explained to Hibiki who Tommy was and why he had come. He also told Tommy it would be best for Hibiki to explain the situation to Aiko. He felt it would be beneficial for the family to think about all of this and meet with Tommy the next day, if they so desired.

Aiko returned with a tray upon which was a tea pot and four tiny teacups. She sat the tray on the table, and stood behind Hibiki. His mask never changed as he began to pour the tea into the cups. Tommy had no clue as to what Hibiki was thinking.

Back in the Jeep, as they were returning to the

hotel, the mayor's aide said he was sure they would want to speak with Tommy again. Tommy ate in the hotel restaurant that evening. He did not sleep well that night. After shaving the next morning, he heard a knock at his door. It was the aide to the mayor. He said the family wanted to speak with him. He also said the former fiancé to Hioto wanted to speak with him. Tommy thought, *So, she is still alive.* But where was Hioto's father, who had written the letter?

At about ten o'clock, Tommy and the aide arrived at the Sato home. Again, Aiko opened the door. Inside, Hibiki was seated at the table, as was an attractive, petite, young woman. Even though the picture was almost ten years old, Tommy immediately recognized her as the girl in the watch. Tommy and the aide were invited to sit, and tea was poured into cups for them. After an introduction to the young lady, whose name was Mika, Tommy cleared his throat and began to speak.

He spoke a sentence or two at a time in order to let the aide translate. Tommy spoke about how sorry he was for this family. And how sorry he was that he had been the one responsible for Hioto not coming home. He could not bear to use the word "kill." He then blurted out, "Please forgive me!" A tear was forming in the corner of his eye. And he didn't have a handkerchief on him. He wiped at it with the back of his hand and then with his sleeve.

To his great surprise, Mika spoke directly to Tommy in very good English. She said she could only speak for herself, but that she forgave him. She said she understood that it was an act that was done in the heat of battle.

Tommy sat with his mouth slightly open in shock. He had no idea this young lady could speak such flawless English.

She then began to translate for the Satos. They, too, had come to grips with the death of this boy. They were so happy to get some of his things back and to finally put closure to his death. Painful, yes. But they, too, understood that people do horrible things in war. As she said this, she dropped her gaze into her teacup. A tear was rolling down her lovely cheek.

Tommy was thinking, "I sure would like to take her in my arms and hug her." But he knew that would not be acceptable. So he simply said, "I am so sorry." He arose from his kneeling position at the table and whispered, "I have to go now. Please don't hate me."

Back at his hotel room, Tommy rearranged all his things on the dresser and in his suitcase, just to have something to do. A little later, he went to the lobby and asked if there were any small shops where he could buy some souvenirs. He was directed to a small open air booth on one of the side streets. He bought some wooden paperweights shaped like tigers for the boys, bracelets for each of the girls, and a beautiful butterfly pin for his mother. He would be leaving in just a couple of days, so he thought perhaps later he would walk around and see some sights.

Returning to his room, Tommy found a note stuck in his door. It was from Mika; she said she wanted to see him again. She said she would return at five that evening.

At four thirty that evening, Tommy was seated in the lobby with his eyes glued to the entrance. Promptly at five, Mika entered the lobby. She spied Tommy and came to him smiling. She only bowed slightly and extended her hand to him. She not only knew English, she was learning the American ways. Mika said she knew of a small café within walking distance that served American food. Tommy said that would be great.

As they ate that evening, they talked about how

their lives and their expectations had been changed by the war. Tommy asked Mika if she had found love again. She said, "No, so many men my age never returned from the war." She said she would likely be like so many other girls her age. She would live out her life without a husband and without a child.

She also told Tommy that she had been chosen by Hiroto's family for him to marry. She said she supposed she had loved him, but only because she was supposed to love him.

She said, "I like the western way of pairing off. Meeting, dating, falling in love, and getting married because you both want to. Not just because your families think they know what is best." Tommy asked her about Hiroto's father. She said, "He took sick and died shortly after he received notice from the war department that Hiroto was killed in action." She went on, "Some said he died of a broken heart. He had such wonderful plans for his only son."

Tommy said, almost to himself, "Another casualty of war."

Tommy found himself fascinated by this very pretty young lady, Mika. He wanted to know her better and in typical American boldness, told her so.

Mika smiled and took his hand in hers. She said, "I would like to know more about you as well."

After a couple of hours walking around Tokyo, Mika said she needed to go home. Her father was in failing health and she needed to check on him.

Tommy insisted on escorting her home. They took a bus from Tokyo to Bancho. They walked to her house which was at the edge of town, almost in the country.

On this walk, Tommy also learned that Mika had taken off a couple of days from her job at the American embassy. She had been fortunate enough to land that job right after it opened back up. It was there she learned to speak fluent English and more about American customs.

She had also learned much from watching American movies, which were now popular in Japan. She stopped him at the front door, and he took her hand to shake it. She touched his cheek softly with her left hand, stood on tiptoes and kissed him tenderly on the mouth. Then she said, "I will be in touch with you tomorrow. Check in the lobby for a message." Nothing else was said as she slipped inside.

Tommy rode back to Tokyo with nothing but this beautiful young lady, Mika, on his mind. He loved her name, but he wondered if she would mind if he called her "Mike" instead. He just thought that would be cute, to call her Mike. The next two days went too fast for Tommy. He spent a lot of time with Mika because she insisted.

The day came for his departure back to America. He had a farm to manage and work to do. But he found Mika in his waking thoughts, and occasionally in his dreams. He also began to sleep better than he had slept since he was a kid. It is amazing what forgiveness does for a person.

Tommy and "Mike," as he now called her, wrote to each other several times a week. He told her all about the farm, his family, and the Bear Creek Church. She seemed very interested in everything he wrote. She asked so many questions that he filled pages and pages with answers.

Then one night as he sat down to write, he thought, *This is silly. I really wish Mika was here with me.*

He had always signed his letters to her with "Love you, Tommy." That night, he wrote, "Dearest darling Mika, I want you to know I love you more than I have ever loved any other girl in my life. I want you for my wife if you will have me." He asked her if she could pull any strings or find out how she might be able to come to him.

Strings really did not need to be pulled to get Mika to come to America. A law passed in 1947 had opened up a way. But a Japanese person would have to have a sponsor. They would also need to have a skill. This would make things so much easier for Tommy and Mika, for she was fluent in English and Japanese. Interpreters were needed in several federal agencies.

Tommy made a plea to the Bear Creek Church of Christ to help him sponsor Mika. There were no vocal protests, with only one or two who had some silent reservations about this.

In a letter, Mika said she did not want to come while her father was still living. But he was very sick with an inoperable tumor in his intestine. The doctor called it cancer.

In the meantime, Tommy saved his money. He would not ask the church for financial help this time. He only asked that they give moral support and prayers to get her to America.

On January 3, 1951, Tommy opened a letter

from Mika. Her father had passed away on December 15, 1950. She said she was now free to come to the United States. She would begin the proceedings. The wheels of government grind slowly. On July 1, 1951, Mika was cleared to come to America. She had her sponsors: Tommy, his family, and the Bear Creek congregation.

Tommy met Mika as she came down the gangplank of that large passenger ship at San Diego. She looked as fresh and as beautiful as a rose in the morning dew. Tommy picked her up in his arms and held her tight for the first time. She kissed him as he held her. She hadn't brought many pieces of luggage with her. All she had was a suitcase, an overnight bag, and a large trunk. The next to last leg of the trip was by train.

Jake Jennings met them at the train station in Indianapolis. They laughed and talked all the way home. As they rolled up in Jake's old Plymouth, there was a banner on the porch of the farmhouse—*Welcome home, Mika!* It was a joyful time that evening at supper. Everyone wanted to wait on Mika. Finally, Tommy said, "Okay folks, Mika has had a long journey. She needs her beauty sleep." To which, everyone laughed and the brothers both exclaimed, "No way!"

Mika was moved into the bedroom with the girls. The sisters were thrilled with this arrangement. It was a tight fit, but Tommy reminded the family that this is only temporary. Besides that, Mika was used to small rooms. The houses in Japan are tiny by comparison to the large farmhouse with its cavernous rooms.

The Neal family was reminded that in small town America, people are sometimes suspicious of strangers. Especially suspicious of strangers who were your enemy less than a decade before. However, things went better than expected in the small town of Frankfort.

At Bear Creek Church of Christ, there were some murmurings when Mika came into the building on Tommy's arm. She turned to the congregation and smiled when Jake had her stand to introduce her. But the smiles returning to her seemed more like grinning masks. Later, just outside the front door as she met individual people, many seemed surprised by her command of the English language. Actually, she captured them with her graciousness and humility.

On the way home, Mika had many questions about God, Christ, the church, and what was meant by grace. Tommy did his best to explain. Mika had actually never worshipped anything in her life except the Emperor of Japan when she was young. The horrible war had clouded her mind with doubt and disappointment. She realized the Emperor was only a man. Why had he agreed with the military to join a fight they could never win?

However, Mika had found she actually enjoyed the service at Bear Creek even though she didn't understand much of Jake's jargon.

She understood love and forgiveness. She was not so sure about mercy and grace. She could not understand a loving father allowing his son to be horribly mistreated and to be nailed to a cross. If he was such a powerful God, why didn't he prevent this?

Tommy did his best to explain these terms to Mika. Ruth had a better plan. She asked Mika if she would like to help her and the girls with the household chores. Mika was eager to pitch in. Ruth used this time with Mika to answer some of her questions about Christianity. She used illustrations from cooking and cleaning to teach Mika about

Jesus and the church. By the end of the week, Mika had grasped some of these doctrines.

The next Sunday during Sunday School, the teacher, John Cummings, gave Mika a Bible from the class. It had her name printed in gold on the front cover. She proudly clutched it to her heart. During the class, Tommy helped her find the scripture.

On the way home, she vowed that she would read some from her new Bible every day. She wanted to know more about Tommy's religion. Because, she told herself, it had made him into such a kind, compassionate, and loving man. He was so unlike many of the Japanese men she knew.

Each evening that week, after the dishes were done, Mika, Tommy, Ruth, and the girls sat down and began to plan the wedding. After a few nights of this, Tommy said, "I know what I am supposed to do, so you girls just go ahead and make all the arrangements." Mika asked, "What do you mean, you know what you're supposed to do?" Tommy grinned a huge grin and held up his checkbook. The room erupted in laughter.

The wedding at Bear Creek Church of Christ

was said to be one of the most beautiful weddings held there in recent years. The whole congregation turned out, and many others from the community as well. The old building was full when Jake led Tommy and his brother out of a side room to the stage. Tommy's high school principal, Paul Christian, agreed to walk Mika down the aisle. He had a lot to do with her even being in America.

Perhaps the most distinguished guest was Dr. Katsu Ito from Indiana University. He came at the invitation of Tommy and Mika. At the reception, Dr. Ito said he had wanted to meet the girl in the watch. He commented that she was much more beautiful than her picture.

Dr. Ito and Mika chatted in their native tongue about the Japanese empire of the 1930s as compared with the new Japan. In many ways, Japan was better and stronger than she had ever been. Dr. Ito was still a little old-fashioned in his thinking that some things had changed too swiftly. But even he could see that a strong bond had developed between two former enemies.

Dr. Ito also noted in his journal what he had observed. He hoped he could teach his students what he had learned: the love between a man and woman from two very different cultures had the power to heal many wounds and cover many scars.

After a three-day honeymoon at Niagara Falls, the happy couple returned to the sedate routine of farm life in Middle America.

Tommy had measured off a piece of land on the farm on which to build a house for Mika and himself. It was about an acre with a stand of silver maple trees on it. He was able to swing a loan at First Bank and Trust of Clinton County. He contacted a builder with whom he had graduated, Ben Woods. Ben had served in the Army Corp of Engineers during the war.

Upon his discharge, he had attended Purdue University for two years, taking mechanical engineering. However, he realized he liked working with his hands better than designing things. He thus started his own construction company.

He told Tommy if he and his brothers wanted to assist him, he could build the new house faster and cheaper. It was after the corn was planted, and so they would have at least a month before haying season started. If the weather held, they would have a good start on it before August.

In the meantime, Mika joined Tommy in his loft

room in the attic. It was a joyful time those first few weeks of marriage. The new house was going up, and the farm work was going as planned. Both were up early in the morning. Mika even helped with the milking each morning before Tommy went off to work on the house. She loved the farm.

Ben said he actually only needed two laborers for the carpentry. So one of the boys and Tommy worked on the house, and the other boy did the farming. They switched out from week to week.

In the late fall of 1953, Tommy and Mika Neal moved into their new home. The next Sunday at church, Preacher Jennings announced that the church was going to give the couple what he called "a pounding" as a housewarming.

On Wednesday evening, all the members of the church brought food with which to stock the Neals' pantry and refrigerator. A pound of butter, five pounds of flour, cornmeal, and sugar. Twenty pounds of potatoes, ten pounds of onions, and so forth. Thus, they received "a pounding."

Tommy got up in front of the church on the next Sunday and said, "I have always heard the expression 'my cup runneth over.' But, folks, my pantry and storeroom runneth over. Thank you all."

Tommy came home from picking corn one late fall day and Mika met him at the door as always. However, on this evening she leaped up and wrapped her arms around Tommy's neck and her legs around his waist as she lifted herself from the floor. He caught her up in his arms, and their lips met and lingered for what seemed like a full minute.

Tommy said, "Wow, what was that all about?" as he gently set her on the couch. She whispered in his ear, "We're having a baby!" Tommy plopped down, slowly shook his head, and with a quizzical look, said, "What did you say?" This time, she nibbled on his earlobe and whispered very slowly this time, "I said we are having a baby." He took her in his arms, held her close, and with his lips, he gently brushed her beautiful, oriental face, before coming to rest firmly on her lips.

It was the happiest time Tommy could actually ever remember. It was like all the Christmases he had ever had all rolled up into one. Over and over he said, "I am going to be a daddy ... I am going to be a daddy."

That night after supper he told Mika he was

going over to the homeplace for a while. It was less than half a mile and it was a crisp moonlit night, so he walked. He quietly slipped into the barn and found the stall where he had sometimes found his dad on his knees during tough times.

Tommy fell on his knees in his father's sanctuary and talked to the Lord. Tommy said many things to God in a tone that sounded like he was just talking to a friend. He thanked God for this little baby. He cared not if it was a boy or a girl. He only wanted to be a good father like his own dad. As he closed his prayer, he said, "Jesus, I'm scared. I'm as scared as the times I hit the beaches during the war. Help me, Lord, please help me. Amen."

On a hot July day as Tommy was loading bales of hay into the barn, Jean came running from the house. She was so excited she could hardly speak. "Tommy! Mika needs you at home, right now!" Jumping from the wagon, Tommy ran to his truck and raised a cloud of dust as he spun out of the barnyard.

Tommy found his mother kneeling beside Mika, holding her hand and soothing her with a cool, wet washcloth on her head. The pains had started only an hour ago, but they were now less than ten minutes apart.

Tommy took one look but said nothing as he scooped Mika up in his arms and carried her to his truck. He thought to himself, "*She is not as heavy as a bale of green hay.*" The Ford skidded sideways as he roared out onto the gravel road. Baptist Hospital was ten miles away in Frankfort.

Tommy paced the floor in the waiting room. He looked at the clock every few minutes, but time seemed to have stopped. Slowly the minute hand moved ... one hour ... two hours. Finally, at eight fifteen that evening, an older, smiling maternity nurse filled the doorway of the waiting room. She motioned for him to follow her down the hall and into a rather cramped room.

There lay his beautiful Mika with a tiny bundle under her left arm, close to her heart. Tommy kissed her gently on the forehead. "Are you okay, sweetheart?" She just smiled, nodded, and softly whispered, "Oh yes, I'm just fine." She reached and pulled the blanket down slightly. A tuft of coal black hair stood up from that tiny head. Tommy gazed into a rather delicate, oriental-shaped face with slightly slanted eyes, which were barely open. The nurse turned and spoke as she prepared to leave the room. "He is a beautiful baby."

That night in his father's sanctuary at the old barn, Tommy once again bent his gangly frame down in the hay. "God, as you well know, in a time of war, I took the life of a fellow human being. Lord, I looked into his lifeless eyes and at that moment I hated a man I did not even know. But, Lord, you know I repented and have begged your forgiveness. I believe you have. Now, Lord, by your mighty creative power, I have brought a new life into this world. I looked into my baby boy's eyes and loved as I have never loved before. And, Lord, I am now at peace with myself. Thank you, Lord Jesus. Amen."

ABOUT THE AUTHOR

Born in 1937 during the Great Depression, Phil Emmert was raised near Lebanon, Indiana. At the age of thirty-three, he left a well-paying job with Dow Chemical Company, sold his little farm, and took his family to Knoxville, Tennessee, where he enrolled and completed four years at Johnson Bible College (Johnson University).

Phil preached in several small congregations in Tennessee and North Carolina. At the same time, he held several different secular jobs to supplement his income. As a school counselor, he wrote weekly inspirational thoughts for teachers and staff.

At age seventy-seven, he published his first book, *When War Was Heck*, followed by *The Afterglow of War: Lessons Learned*, which were reflections from his childhood and teen years. Phil of late has changed his focus toward more Christian-based stories. *The Overcomers*, *America Rebooted*, and this newest one, *The Reprieve*.

Phil acknowledges that he was a poor student in high school and even later in college. He often jokes that he wishes his teachers and professors could see him now. However, through his varied life experiences, he has become an appealing communicator and storyteller.

Phil and his wife Bea live in Washington, North Carolina. They drive fifty-five miles twice a week to a neighboring county where he still preaches in a small congregation.

You can learn more about Phil's book collection by visiting his publisher's site:
www.thewordverve.com/authors/Phil-Emmert

For inquiries and comments, please email the publisher at writenow@thewordverve.com.

Reviews are so important to our authors. Please take a moment to provide feedback at one of the online book retailers or on our website www.thewordverve.com. Or even by email! We look forward to hearing your thoughts

www.ingramcontent.com/pod-product-compliance
Lightning Source LLC
Chambersburg PA
CBHW070514170726
48291CB00008B/2739

* 9 7 8 1 9 4 8 2 2 5 6 6 3 *